Ben, his Helmet and the Teacher Switch

Written by Nelle Frances
Illustrated by Mark Ambroz

1

Publishing of this title has been made possible by the Caloundra City Council, Queensland, and the Arts Council, Queensland.

© Janelle Wall 2008

First published 2008.

Published by Janelle Wall trading as Nelle Frances
ABN 40 090 061 728
20 Buderim Street, Caloundra, Qld 4551, Australia
www.nellefrances.com
www.aspergerchild.com

Edited by Heather King, 2007
Text copyright © Janelle Wall, 2008
Illustrations copyright © Mark Ambroz, MAD Design 2007
Printed by Watson Ferguson, 1/655 Toohey Road, Salisbury, Qld 4107, Australia

ISBN 978-0-646-47244-7

National Library of Australia
Cataloguing-in-Publication entry
Frances, Nelle, 1963 - .
Ben, His Helmet and the Teacher Switch

Dedication

The road travelled holds the fondest memories when traversed with friends.

Thank you to my companions on the journey:-

Diane, for justifying the trip
Lyn, for organising the trip
Dave, for being level-headed on the road
John, for being there when we were weary
Leiza and Trevor, for bringing passion to the journey

May the highways ahead of us be smooth.

4

Chapter 1

Ben is 8 years and 9 months old. He's in Grade 3 at Bluehills Primary School, which he thinks is a silly name for a school, because even though it's on a hill, everybody knows that hills aren't blue!

Ben has a special helmet, which he takes everywhere with him. He knows that it used to belong to aliens from another planet, but the most exciting thing Ben has discovered about his helmet is that it's magic! It whispers to him, answering his questions and solving his problems. He calls it his "tell-me" helmet.

Today is Monday, and when Ben arrived at school he put his bag on the port rack, and took his helmet inside to the quiet area at the back of the classroom.

When Ben went outside to wait for the bell, he noticed something on the ground near the port rack. He went over for a closer look – it was a digital watch! What was it doing on the ground? Had someone lost it? There wasn't time before the bell went to ask everyone in the school if they'd lost their watch, so Ben decided to take it to the office.

The office had four adults and two school children waiting inside to be helped. It was very noisy, with telephones ringing and people talking to each other. Three teachers were walking into the office and one was rushing out. Ben waited at the back, with one hand covering an ear, and the other hand holding the watch. Snippets of conversation floated over to him.

"Good morning, Bluehills Primary School, Libby speaking........"

"Katie spilt her milkshake on a library book last night......"

"Mr. Pellum will be away on Thursday.... Yes, I'll let him know."

Ben stopped moving and stood very still. Why was Mr. Pellum going to be away on Thursday? Where was he going? Who would teach them? Ben felt sick in the stomach, and his heart thump, thump, thumped in his chest.

"Ben, what can I do for you this morning?" Libby, the school secretary, asked.

Ben couldn't think why he'd come to the office. He looked at Libby and blinked.

"What have you got in your hand, Ben? Is it something for the 'Lost and Found'?" enquired Libby gently.

Aah! That's what he'd been doing!

"Yes," replied Ben enthusiastically, "I found this digital watch near the Grade 3 port rack and thought someone must have lost it. I didn't have time to ask everyone in the school if they'd lost their watch, so I've brought it here."

Libby smiled at Ben, took the watch and put it in a special drawer, and thanked Ben for handing it in. She wrote his name down on an "Honesty is the Best Policy" list of children who had handed things in. Each week at Assembly they picked one person's name out of a hat. That person got a free iceblock from the tuckshop as a reward for being honest.

Just then the bell rang!

"Oh no, I'd better hurry to get to class. I don't like to be late," worried Ben, as he raced out the door.

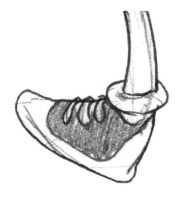
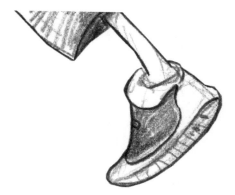

Chapter 2

In the classroom the children sat together on the floor. Mr. Pellum called their names one by one, and the children answered, "Good morning". He told them they would be learning about plants this week, and examining the different leaf shapes and textures of the plants in Science. They would use leaf shapes for "stamping" pictures in Art, and they would be thinking of "describing" words for leaves this morning for their writing activity.

Ben's hand shot up. He remembered to wait until Mr. Pellum invited him to speak, "Yes, Ben?"

"Where are you going on Thursday, and who's going to teach us?" asked Ben with a frown.

"Thankyou for reminding me, Ben. Class, I'll be away on Thursday; I'm taking a group of children to compete in the Cross-Country District Finals. Mr. Brown will be coming in to teach you for the day. You'll be continuing your work with leaves, and completing activities that I've set for you," replied Mr. Pellum. "I expect you to listen to Mr. Brown and show him how well our class works together," Mr. Pellum explained.

Ben's hand shot up again.

"But I don't know Mr. Brown, and I like the way you teach us; I don't want to change teachers," blurted Ben in a rush.

"Don't worry, Ben. Let's cross that bridge when we come to it, OK? Back to your seats, everyone, and we'll start thinking about some describing words for leaves."

Once Ben was back in his seat his hands felt sweaty, and his heart was thump, thump, thumping again. The fluorescent lights seemed to be *BURNING* into his eyes. There were no bridges to cross between school and home. What bridge was Mr. Pellum talking about? Ben started rocking on his chair.

"Perhaps you need some time out, Ben," suggested Mr. Pellum.

Chapter 3

Ben snatched his helmet off the shelf,
put it on and sat down on a beanbag.
With his helmet in place and the visor
closed, the noise of the other children
became quieter, the lights stopped
"burning" his eyes and his thumping heart

slowed down a little. He could hardly hear the clock tick, tick, ticking. Ben began to relax.

"Shoo, shoo, shoosh," the tiny voice of his helmet whispered. "I know you are worried about Mr. Pellum being away on Thursday."

"Yes," replied Ben gruffly. "And I don't know what bridge he's talking about. The only bridge I've ever crossed is the one near Aunt Jane's house, but that's far away from here!"

"Shoo, shoo, shoosh," the little voice soothed. " *Let's cross that bridge when we come to it* means not getting upset about something until it happens. Mr. Pellum doesn't want you to worry about him being away on Thursday."

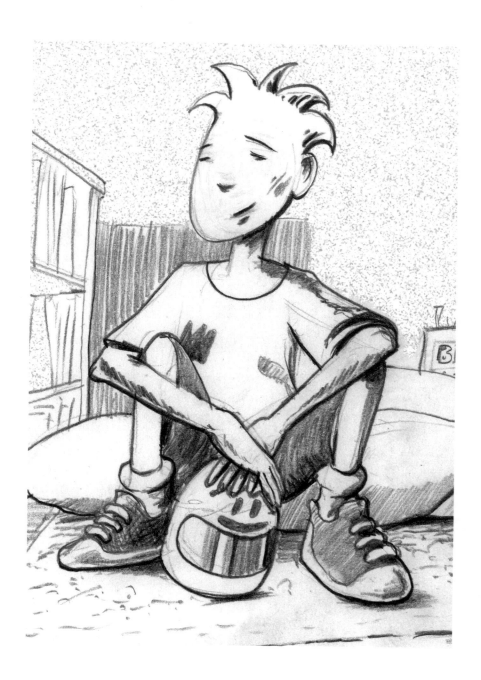

"Oh...but I can't stop thinking about it," said Ben softly.

"Then you should talk to Mr. Pellum...I'm sure he'll find a solution," his helmet advised him wisely.

Mr. Pellum came over to the quiet area and sat down on the other beanbag. He smiled at Ben. Ben took off his helmet.

"Tell me what's bothering you, Ben," invited Mr. Pellum.

"Well, I don't want Mr. Brown to teach us on Thursday. I don't know how he does things...and he doesn't know I have a helmet and about the quiet area or anything! I'm not ready for a new teacher!" moaned Ben.

23

"Hmm," said Mr. Pellum, "I can see you're worried about Thursday. I have an idea that might help you feel better about changing teachers for the day. Can you wait until tomorrow for me to share it with you?" asked Mr. Pellum.

"Well...I'll try to," answered Ben hesitantly, "and I know what you meant when you said *Let's cross that bridge when we come to it* now. At first I thought you were talking about the bridge near Aunt Jane's house, but that's too far away."

Mr. Pellum laughed and Ben laughed too.

Chapter 4

The next morning when Ben was taking his helmet into the classroom, he saw that Mr. Pellum was already sitting at his desk.

"Good morning, Ben. When you've put your helmet away come over here and I'll share my idea with you," said Mr. Pellum.

Ben joined Mr. Pellum at his desk.

"Ben, I've written a story for you. It's called a Social Story™*, and it's entitled 'On Thursday, Mr. Brown Will Be Our Teacher'. Will you read it with me?" asked Mr. Pellum.

Ben looked at the page and read out loud.

"On Thursday, Mr. Pellum will be away.

Mr. Brown will teach our class. Mr. Brown teaches at lots of different schools.

Mr. Brown will have a list of work for us to do.

Mr. Brown will know about my helmet and using the quiet area when I need to.

Thursday might be different from usual, because Mr. Brown may do things differently. Doing things differently can make school more interesting. Some things might even be better.

I will try to do my work the same as I always do.

Mr. Pellum will be back on Friday."

Ben looked at the pictures on the page. He read the story again to himself. He turned the page. There was a story called "Fire Drill", and on the next page one called "Going On Excursion".

"We can add to your stories all the time, and create a whole book of stories just for you. Then we can read the stories each day. That way you can get ready for change and things won't take you by surprise," explained Mr. Pellum.

"OK" said Ben, "if you think it will help."

"I'm sure it will help!" replied Mr. Pellum.

"One more thing, Ben," Mr. Pellum went on, "why don't we start using a hand signal when you need to go to the quiet area? That way we can just signal each other during the day."

"That might work," said Ben. "What should we have as the signal?"

"Well, you could use a 'thumbs up', or maybe an 'OK' sign, where you make an 'O' with your thumb and index finger," said Mr. Pellum.

"I like the OK sign; can we try that?" replied Ben.

They agreed on the OK sign, and talked about how Ben had to make sure Mr. Pellum saw the signal, and how Mr. Pellum could just nod his head or walk to Ben's desk and make the signal on the desk with his hand. It would be like having a secret signal! And on Thursday when Mr. Brown was teaching their class, Ben could use the signal with him.

So that day when Ben wanted to go to the quiet area, he waited until Mr. Pellum was looking at him, and then he made the OK signal with his thumb and index finger. Mr. Pellum nodded and kept speaking to the class. Ben went to the quiet area and read the stories Mr. Pellum had written for him. That afternoon he asked if he could take the book home to show his mum.

"Yes, that's a great idea! Be sure to bring it back to school tomorrow so you can read it again," answered Mr. Pellum.

By Wednesday afternoon, Ben had read the stories eight times! He found he enjoyed reading them over and over. And when he thought about Mr. Brown being their teacher on Thursday, his heart didn't start thump, thump, thumping at all!

Chapter 5

On Thursday morning the children sat on the floor together, and Mr. Brown called their names one by one. They greeted him with "Good morning!" He made them laugh when he tried to say some of their last names! Mr. Brown had nice rectangular-shaped glasses.

He told them that this afternoon they would be making a collage of leaves for their Art activity, and this morning they would be writing a "Who Am I?" about themselves, using describing words, and he would try to guess who each one was! That sounded like fun to Ben!

During the day the children sometimes had to remind Mr. Brown about things like when to send the lunch orders down to the canteen and what time lunch was. He thanked them for their help. He didn't mind when Ben made the "signal" and went to the quiet area; he just smiled and nodded at Ben.

At the end of the day, when Ben was just finishing his leaf collage, Mr. Brown came over to him.

"I think you are a very responsible student, Ben; you go to the quiet area when you need to. Well done!" he said quietly.

Ben smiled at him. He couldn't wait to tell Mr. Pellum tomorrow – he hadn't minded Mr. Brown teaching them at all. In fact, even though the day had been different, it had been fun! Maybe his Social Story™ book had helped after all.

That afternoon when Mum picked him up he told her all about his day and the things he'd done.

"...and you know, Mum, it really *is* a magical helmet."

"Yes," said Mum, "so you keep telling me."

*A Social Story is a technique developed by Carol Gray. © Gray, C. (1994) Social Stories and Comic Strip Conversations - Unique Methods to Improve Social Understanding. Future Horizons Inc. For more information visit www.thegraycenter.org/socialstories.cfm

The Social Story™ used in "Ben, His Helmet and the Teacher Switch" is an example only, and not to be used as a support strategy for any individual. Social Stories™ should be constructed by following the formula described in "Social Stories and Comic Strip Conversations" and created to suit individual circumstances.

Leaf Facts

Not all leaves are green.

The green color in leaves is from a chemical called chlorophyll.

Leaves convert sunlight to energy in a process called photosynthesis.

Photosynthesis is the process plants use to produce oxygen.

Leaves produce oxygen and carbohydrates.

Leaves are the primary food-manufacturing organ of a plant.

A leaf consists of a stalk (petiole) and a blade (leaf).

The petiole is the thin stalk that connects the leaf blade to the stem.

The leaf blade is veined. The central vein is called the midrib.

The outer edge of a leaf blade is called the margin.

The tip of a leaf is called the apex.

Other pigments besides chlorophyll that give leaves color are:-

- Carotenoids – orange-red and yellow
- Anthocyanins – red, purple and blue
- Tannins – brown
- White – results from lack of pigments

The leaves of some plants drop to the ground during autumn/fall.

Cactus spines are a type of modified leaf.

Plants use leaves for protection, climbing, trapping insects, water storage or food storage.

The study of plants is called Botany.

Plants grow continually throughout their life.

Leaf Crossword Puzzle

ACROSS
1 Name for central vein of a leaf
4 The process of converting sunlight to energy
5 The tip of a leaf
6 The primary food-manufacturing organ of a plant
8 Another name for a leaf
9 Produced by leaves

DOWN
1 The outer edge of a leaf blade
2 The stalk that connects the leaf to the stem
3 The study of plants
7 The season when leaves fall to the ground

Leaf Word Builder

g	c	z	s	c	c	f	o	l	t	p	h	w	z	m
r	d	r	p	h	f	o	a	a	u	e	e	o	y	t
e	n	a	h	l	m	a	d	e	v	t	m	i	b	k
e	i	u	o	o	i	j	l	q	l	i	p	d	l	p
n	n	t	t	r	d	y	o	l	f	o	e	k	a	t
x	n	u	o	o	r	g	e	q	u	l	a	e	d	r
g	a	m	s	p	i	o	x	y	g	e	n	s	e	w
e	t	n	y	h	b	z	e	e	b	v	r	t	r	z
n	c	c	n	y	m	a	r	g	i	n	p	a	t	f
e	t	u	t	l	u	c	f	m	g	r	c	l	n	n
r	v	x	h	l	p	j	g	h	y	b	h	k	e	d
g	i	e	e	l	w	e	y	v	e	i	n	b	m	f
y	g	p	s	o	t	x	l	c	m	a	h	r	g	e
q	h	a	i	n	m	b	o	t	a	n	y	y	i	s
o	n	g	s	f	r	e	a	h	m	h	g	e	p	h

Find the hidden words

apex
autumn
blade
botany
chlorophyll
energy
fall
green
leaf

margin
midrib
oxygen
petiole
photosynthesis
pigment
stalk
tannin
vein

43

Leaf Anatomy

Use the Leaf Facts pages to fill in the blank spaces

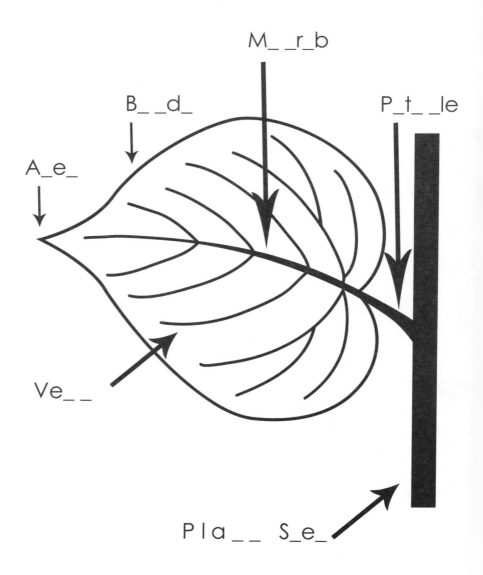

M_ _r_b

B_ _d_

P_t_ _le

A_e_

Ve_ _

Pla_ _ S_e_

Have you read about Ben's other adventures with his helmet? In case you haven't, here are titles of some other books you might enjoy.

Visit

www.aspergerchild.com

About the Author

Nelle Frances was born in Gayndah, Queensland in 1963, well after television was invented. Her skill at story-telling was revealed straight away amongst her five brothers and sisters, and she was soon promoted to the position of "spoilt baby" in the family! After leaving school she spent 15 years in the banking industry, before deciding money wasn't for her. She then went on to educating children... and decided to stay. She now lives in Caloundra, on the Sunshine Coast. Her home is called "Surf Song", and the nearby beach is like her own back yard where she swims, plays and goes for long walks. When she's not racing around after her children, or frantically scribbling notes about new stories, Nelle likes to cook bizarre dishes that she makes up as she goes along and read books with pictures.

About the Illustrator

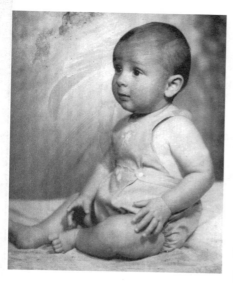

Mark Ambroz was born in Sydney in 1953, which is a very long time ago indeed. He showed early promise in plasticine, crayons and was very good at cutting out. After leaving school he became an architectural draftsman in a big office which he didn't really like, and his mother suggested he might go to art school, because he was so good at crayons and cutting out. He did so and became an artist and so devoted his life to living in abject proverty, apart from a period when he became a high school teacher in Art. He now lives on the Sunshine Coast in Queensland not far from the author, in an old Queensland house. Both the house and the illustrator are currently falling into a happy disrepair.